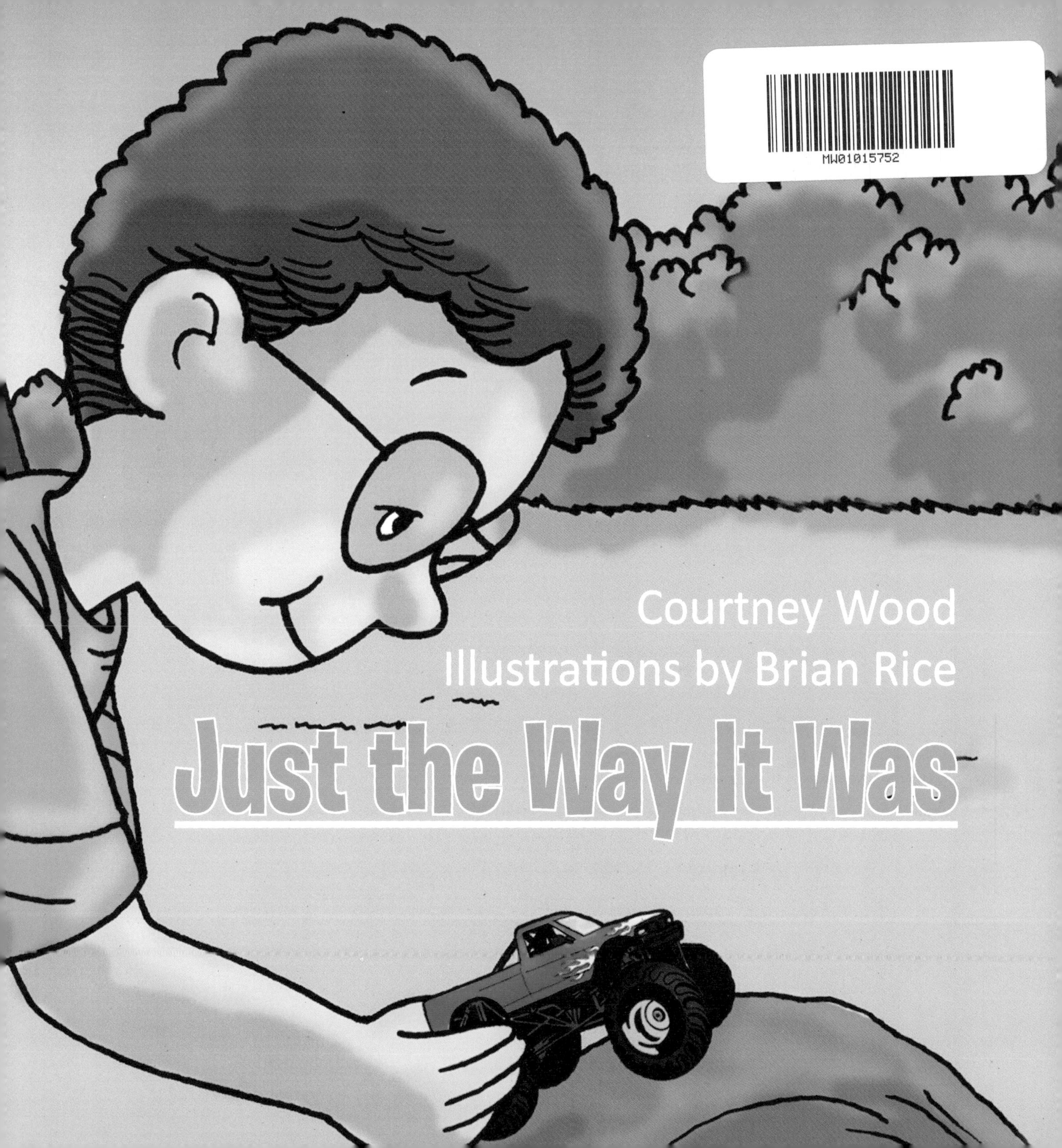
MW01015752
Courtney Wood
Illustrations by Brian Rice
Just the Way It Was

AuthorHouse™
1663 Liberty Drive
Bloomington, IN 47403
www.authorhouse.com
Phone: 1-800-839-8640

Published by AuthorHouse 02/04/2013

ISBN: 978-1-4817-0734-3 (sc)
978-1-4817-0735-0 (e)

Library of Congress Control Number: 2013900836

This book is printed on acid-free paper.

Robert's birthday was a day away; The one thing he had asked his mom for was a giant blue monster truck with flames down the side. Robert's mother, Mary, had looked all over town for the flaming blue monster truck. She had searched through ten different stores before she had found exactly what Robert had asked for.

That night Robert went to bed dreaming about his giant monster truck and all the fun things he would do with it. He would play with it on the swings, in the dirt, and off the jumps in his backyard. In the morning he leapt out of his bed and ran down the stairs. His mother was waiting for him in the kitchen.

"Can I open my presents now?" he shrieked with excitement.

"Yes, Robert, as soon as we finish your birthday breakfast."

"Okay, and then I can open my presents?"

"Yes, Robert."

Breakfast hit the table and Robert had it gobbled up within a matter of seconds. Robert's mother smiled over at him with admiration.

Just as breakfast finished, Robert's family arrived to wish him a happy birthday. It was finally time to open his presents. He tore into them like a tornado.

"Thank you, Aunt Sue, for the Lego, thank you, Uncle Stewart, for the remote control car, and thank you, Aunt Meagan, for superhero pajamas."

It was now time to open his last present from his mother. This was it!

Robert took the package into his hands and softly placed it down in front of him. He untied the bow, pulling the string slowly out to the side. He picked at the tape on the sides of the box and lifted off the top. There it was. The blue monster truck with flames shooting down the sides. He stared at it expressionless. This was not the enormous truck he had asked for. This truck was the size of a tennis ball, not very big at all.

“What do you think Robert?”

“Well . . .” he said, huffing. “It’s so small, in fact, it’s too small.”

That night Robert slept and dreamt of monster trucks. His blue monster truck sat alone on the floor at the end of his bed. He hadn’t played with it once.

In the morning Robert woke up, slipped out of bed, and stretched his arms above his head. He began to walk out of his room, but something out of the corner of his eye stopped him. His monster truck wasn't the size of a tennis ball anymore. In fact, it appeared to have grown.

It was now the size of his mountain bike. *"Mom!"* he yelled.

Mary came bounding up the stairs. "What is it, Robert?"

"It's my monster truck, it's . . . bigger!"

"Oh," said his mother. "I guess you'll want to play with it now?"

"No, it's still too small," he said, running off down the stairs for breakfast.

Robert brushed his teeth, combed his hair, and settled down for bed. He stared at his monster truck sitting at the end of his bed. *Still too small,* he thought. When he got up the next morning, he stretched, rubbed his eyes, and stared with amazement at the end of his bed. His monster truck was no longer the size of a tennis ball or his mountain bike—it was the size of his bed!

"Mom!" he yelled.

His mother came bounding up the stairs. "What is it, Robert?"

"My monster truck—it's even bigger!"

"Oh," said his mother. "I guess you'll want to play with it now?"

"No, it's still too small," he said, running off down the stairs for breakfast. His mother sighed and walked slowly out the door behind him.

Before Robert went to bed, his mother asked him to take his monster truck outside.

“It’s too big to stay in the house now, Robert. You’ll have to take it out!”

Robert rolled his monster truck down the stairs, out the door, and onto the lawn. He rolled it just outside of his bedroom window, where he could see it, just to make sure it was safe. It was still too small to play with.

When Robert got up the next morning he ran straight to his window. His monster truck was not the size of his bed any more—it was as big as a tree.

"Mom!" he yelled.

His mother came bounding up the stairs. "What is it, Robert?"

"My monster truck—it's even bigger!"

"Oh," said his mother. "Surely it's big enough for you to play with now?"

Robert stared out at his monster truck. "No, it's still too small," he said. And off he went out the door and down for breakfast, leaving his mom standing in the door in shock.

Robert went to bed after staring out at his monster truck. It's still too small, he thought as he drifted off to sleep. The next morning Robert heard his mother scream, "Ahhhhh!" Robert looked out the window. His monster truck wasn't the size of a tennis ball, or his bike, or a tree. The tires were as big as the house, the doors were as big as mountains, and the steering wheel was as big as the moon. Robert was so excited that he ran out of the house in his pajamas. Now this is the perfect monster truck. Robert stared up at the truck and said, "I guess I'll have to climb inside!"

After an hour of huffing and puffing, Robert finally reached the driver's seat. The steering wheel was so big he couldn't turn it, the seat was so big he couldn't see out the windshield, and, in fact, Robert couldn't reach anything in the monster truck.

Suddenly the truck began to roll, and there was no stopping it. It ran over a house, it ran over his school, and it almost ran over an old lady walking her dog! Robert didn't know what to do. Finally it came to a screeching halt at the bottom of the hill. Robert slowly climbed down the side of his truck and onto the road where the entire town and his mother awaited him.

That night Robert went to bed sobbing beside his mother. “I didn’t mean for all of that to happen,” he whimpered.

“I know,” said his mother as she tucked him in for bed.

Robert woke up the next morning with a frown on his face. He peered out of his bedroom window, fearing the worst. But he saw nothing. His monster truck wasn't there. It was at the end of his bed.

"Mom!" he yelled.

His mother came bounding up the stairs. "What is it, Robert?"

"My monster truck—it's not the size of a mountain, a tree, or a bike! It's the size of a tennis ball. It's perfect," he squealed, hugging his mom.

Robert played with his monster truck on the swings, in the dirt, and he took it off jumps. He loved his monster truck just the way it was.

CPSIA information can be obtained
at www.ICGtesting.com
Printed in the USA
LVIW020247060313
322862LV00001B

9781481707343